# Curious Creatures

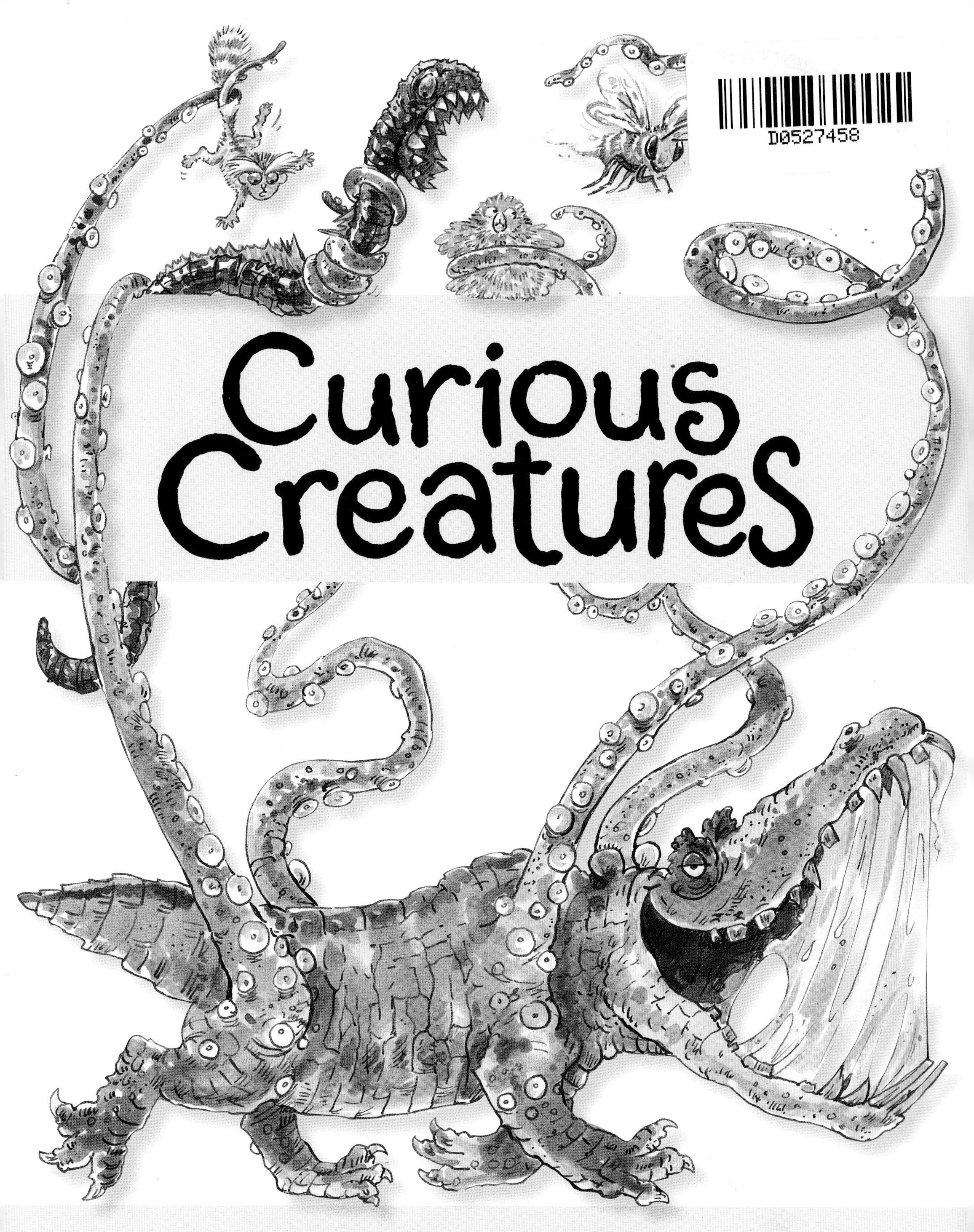

*As imagined by Kevin Price*
*Brought to life by Robin Carter*

KP - For Rudy Amis, who wanted to see a hippocrocopus...
RC - For Christine

Published by KAMA Publishing
19A The Swale, Norwich, NR5 9HE
www.kamapublishing.co.uk

First printed 2013



Paperback ISBN 9780956719652

Printed in Great Britain by
Barnwell Print Ltd, Dunkirk, Aylsham, Norfolk. NR11 6SU

Curious Creatures

# Contents

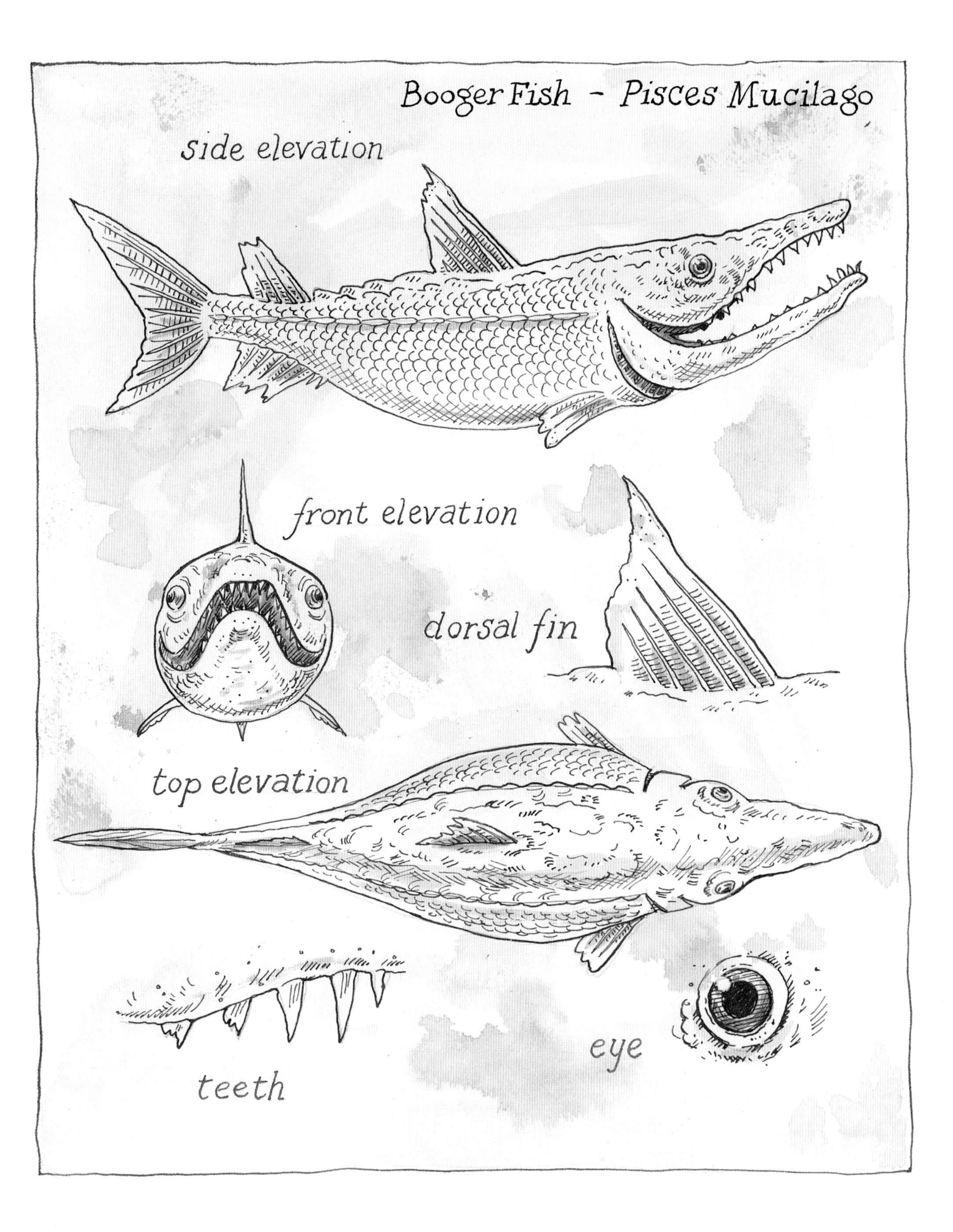
Booger Fish - Pisces Mucilago
side elevation
front elevation
dorsal fin
top elevation
teeth
eye

# The Booger Fish

If you have any sense you'll wish
You never catch a Booger Fish
When you are fishing on the sea –
I'll tell you what one did to me…

It was a cold and windy day
When I set sail from Booger Bay.
It wasn't very long before
I couldn't see the sandy shore.

I hooked my bait, then cast my line
And everything was going fine –
I had no reason to suspect
My fishing voyage could be wrecked.
I felt a tug run up the line
And saw a tail splash through the brine.
It tugged again, I saw a fin,
Then, cheerfully, I reeled it in.
Oh, this was awesome, this was great,
A Booger Fish had snapped the bait!

The Booger Fish was strong and tough,
But I would land it soon enough
(I planned to have it for my lunch
As Booger Fish are good to munch).
I pulled the line with all my might;
The fish put up a fearsome fight.
I gripped the rod with all my strength;
The line now reached its fullest length…
And that was when disaster struck,
While I was left to curse my luck!
The mounting of my rod had split
As I was hanging onto it.

I flew headfirst out of the boat
And, SPLASH! I found myself afloat…
The fish swam off, I trailed behind,
I prayed the sea gods would be kind,
For there's one thing you must be told –
The seawater was FREEZING cold!
The fish turned round and looked at me
With what seemed like malicious glee.

It circled slowly round me, twice,

Then swam my way and, in a trice,

SNAP! SNAP! My yellow oilskin coat

Was disappearing down its throat!

SNAP! SNAP! My boots went down its gullet
(Followed by a shoal of mullet).
SNAP! SNAP! SNAP! My shirt, my hat
(And I was really fond of that!)

SNAP! SNAP! Oh no, oh jeepers, wowzers,
Booger Fish like eating trousers!
Last of all – it's so unfair –
SNAP! SNAP! It ate my underwear!

My naked bottom, with its dimples,
Came alive with big goose pimples.
Numbness spread in fits and starts,
Until it reached my tenderest parts;
Oh man, I tell you, it's the pits
When ice-cold water chills THOSE bits!

The Booger Fish seemed to express
A warm content at my distress.
It swam beside me for a while,
Until I thought I saw it smile.
And then – I don't know what you'll think –
I swear to you, I saw it WINK!
It was enough to make me choke –
The fish had done this for a joke!
It let me float there for a while,
Then swam towards me with great style.
It passed beneath me, flipped its neck
And threw me up onto the deck.
I sailed at speed back to the dock,
While Fishy swam behind to mock.
Now, when I think of this, I wince –
I haven't gone out fishing since.

So, if you're fishing on the sea,
Don't make the same mistake as me.
I was the hunter, so I'd thought,
But it was ME that had been caught.
You've seen how tables can be turned,
So there's a lesson to be learned;
Although it makes a tasty dish,
You shouldn't hunt a Booger Fish
And if you do then take a crew,
Or it might play a prank on you.
If, after all, you're still not scared,
Then make sure that you go prepared.
This is a fact and not a rumour,
Booger Fish have a sense of humour!

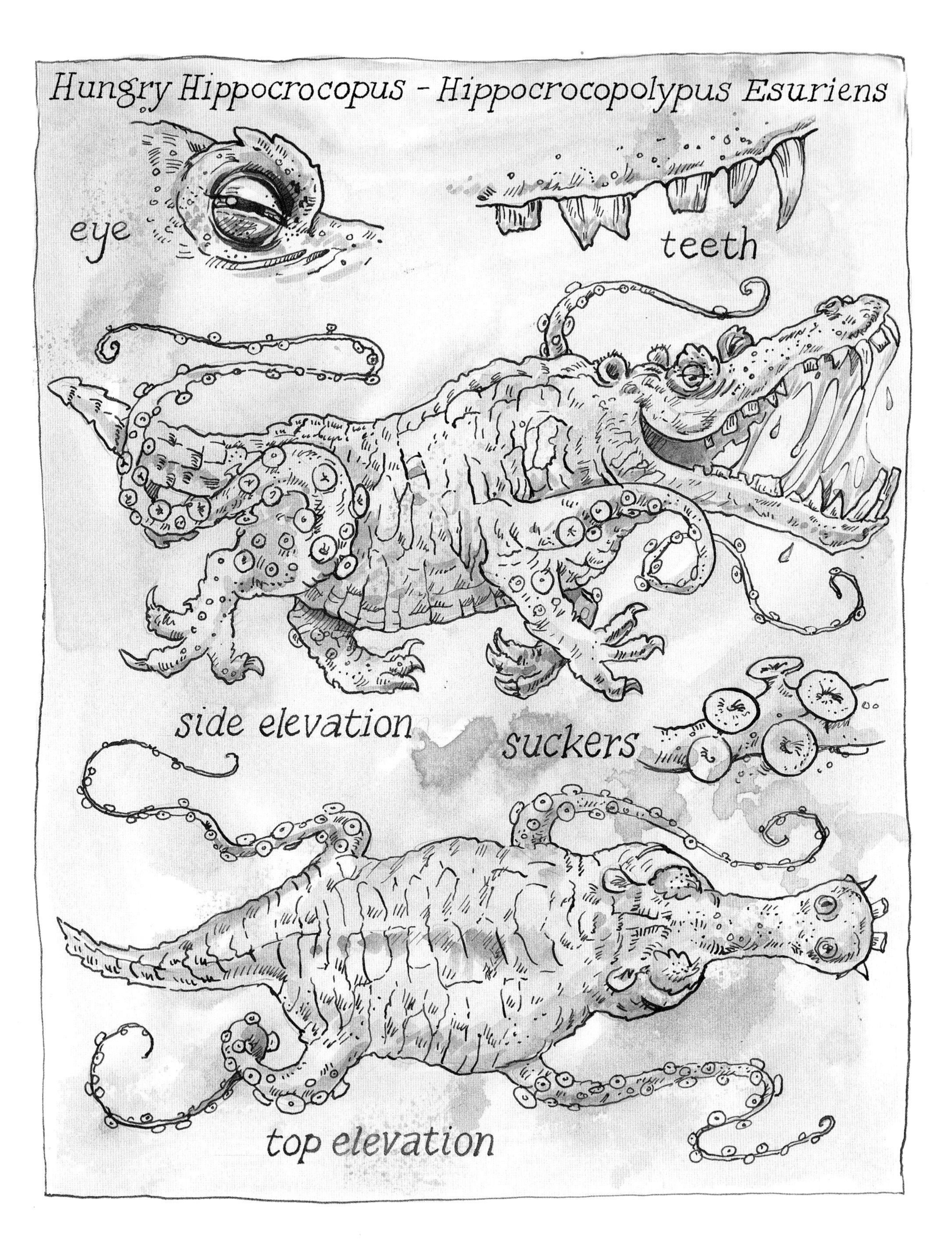
Hungry Hippocrocopus - Hippocrocopolypus Esuriens
eye
teeth
side elevation
suckers
top elevation

# The Hungry Hippocrocopus

If ever you should come across
A Hungry Hippocrocopus,
You mustn't stand around and stare,
JUST GET THE HECK RIGHT OUT OF THERE!
With slimy suckers on his legs,
With breath that smells like rotten eggs,
With jaws that gnash and drool all day –
Take my advice and RUN AWAY!
When one was found in Timbuktu
They took him to a nearby zoo,
Where first he ate a kangaroo
And then he munched a zebra too.

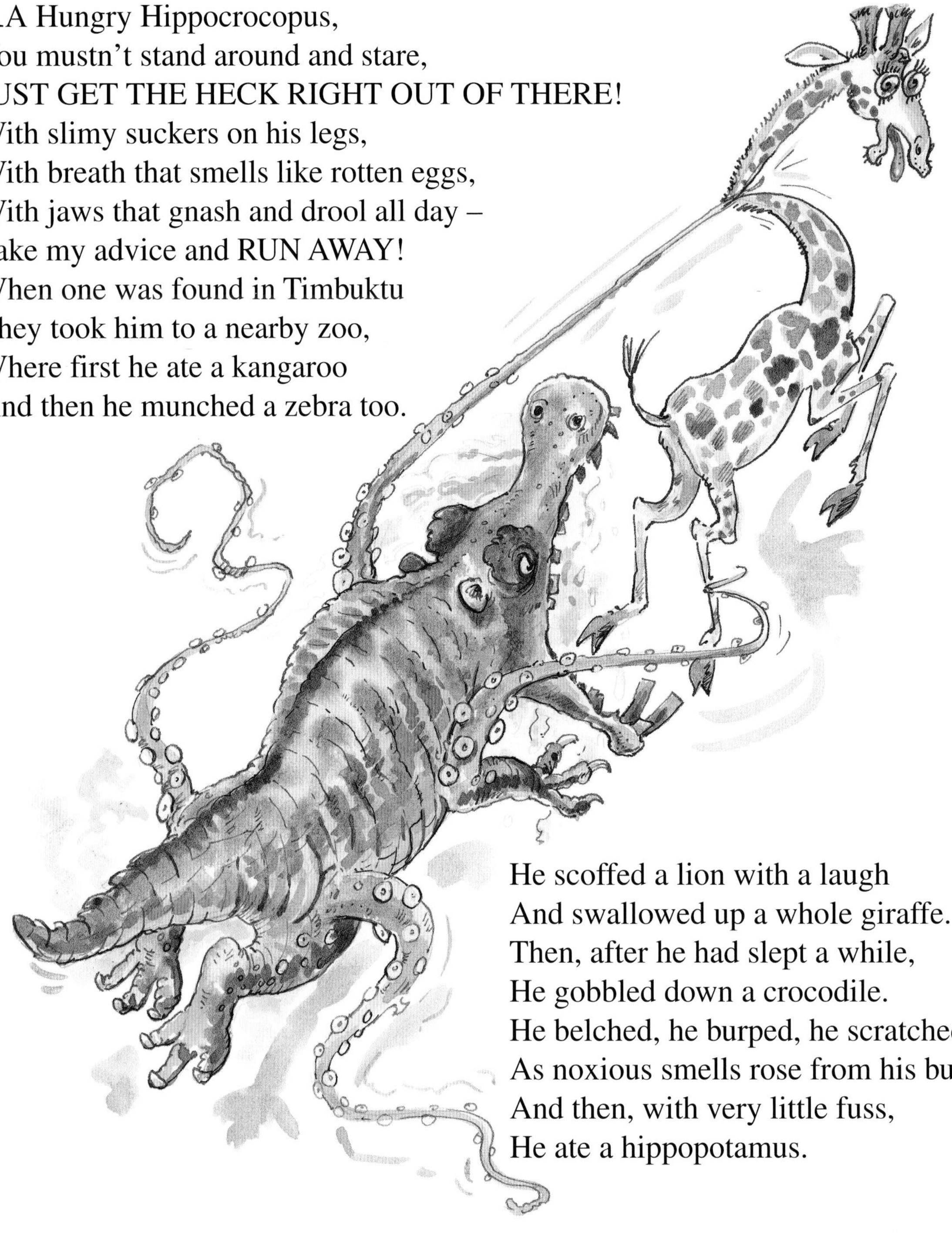

He scoffed a lion with a laugh
And swallowed up a whole giraffe.
Then, after he had slept a while,
He gobbled down a crocodile.
He belched, he burped, he scratched his tum,
As noxious smells rose from his bum.
And then, with very little fuss,
He ate a hippopotamus.

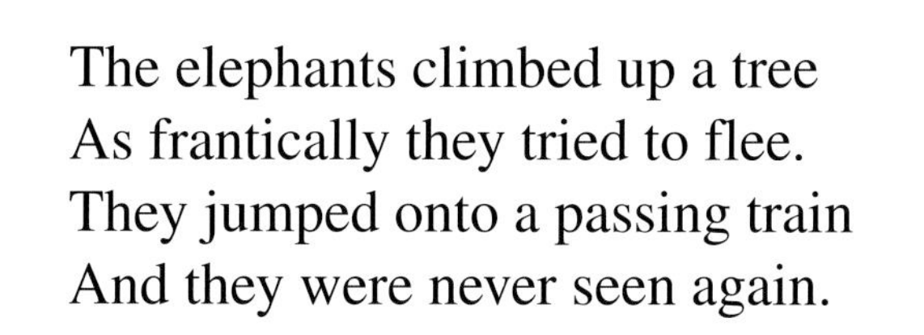

The elephants climbed up a tree
As frantically they tried to flee.
They jumped onto a passing train
And they were never seen again.

The Hungry Hippocrocopus
Then left the zoo and caught a bus,
On which he ravenously tried
To eat the passengers inside.
And next he jumped aboard a plane
To play his dirty tricks again.
He ate the pilot and the crew
(Whose uniforms were navy blue).

He licked his lips and clambered down,
Then walked into the nearest town.
He bounded through the streets with glee
And downed three policemen with his tea.

For weeks he roamed about the land:
He ate an army marching band,
Some cats and dogs, some chocolate bars
And several people driving cars.

But then, one day, he disappeared
And everybody clapped and cheered
And no one knows where he is now,
Or what, or why, or who, or how.

So, if you ever come across
A Hungry Hippocrocopus,
It certainly will not be fun –
**JUST TURN YOURSELF AROUND AND RUN!**

Shrieking Hoolie Boolie Bird - Avis Ejulatus Hooliusboolius
foot
side elevation
wing feather
open beak
top elevation

# the Shrieking Hoolie Boolie Bird

I don't know if you've ever heard
A Shrieking Hoolie Boolie Bird,
But if you haven't then let's see
How loud this little bird can be.
It sucks in air; it swells its chest;
It ruffs the feathers on its breast;
It opens up its tiny beak
To give a shrill and deafening SHRIEK!

Just after this you must beware
A shockwave passing through the air.
Then, from the little creature's rump,
There comes a most unpleasant trump.
Now always, after this event,
Its energy is largely spent.
It settles back into its nest
And needs to have a little rest.

One day, in 1862,
A Great Explorer and his crew
Made anchor on a South Seas isle
And then explored it for a while.
Each sailor had a small glass jar
And walked the island, near and far,
Collecting things and taking notes,
Before returning to their boat.

The Shrieking Hoolie Boolie Bird
Is rarely seen and seldom heard,
But makes its nest upon the ground
And so can easily be found.
It does have wings, but cannot fly
And so, that is the reason why
A sturdy cabin boy named Jim
Was carrying one back with him.
He hacked through jungle foliage
And made his way back to the bridge.

The Great Explorer gave a laugh
And then he took a photograph.
He wrote some notes down on his page,
Then put the bird into a cage.
He put the cage up on a shelf
And meant to keep it for himself.
But never did a sailor make
A more spectacular mistake,

For though he did not know it yet
This bird is not a household pet…

They packed the ship and then set sail.
They saw some dolphins and a whale.
No finer era could there be
To sail a ship upon the sea.

The Great Explorer settled down
At night-time in his dressing gown
And then he started to engage
The little bird inside the cage.
No matter what he did he found
The bird just wouldn't make a sound.

He gave a whistle, then a chirp,
He drank some rum (which made him burp),
He clapped his hands, he played with toys,
But still it wouldn't make a noise.
More rum was drunk and then some more
And soon the man began to snore.

While he was in the depths of sleep
The sly ship's cat began to creep
Towards the cage which held the bird
(But note – its footsteps had been heard!)
It definitely planned to eat
This tantalising tasty treat…

The Shrieking Hoolie Boolie Bird
Went very still…and then it stirred…

It sucked in air; it swelled in size;
It ruffled its feathers; crossed its eyes;
And then it opened up its beak
To give the most humongous SHRIEK!

The shockwave made the whole ship shake,
Which caused the tallest mast to break.
The hull was damaged from within
And seawater came rushing in.
But this was only just the start;
The little bird now did its fart.
The candles burning in the room
Ignited it and **BOOM!**

**BOOM!**

**BOOM!**

The crew were woken from their kip.
A cry went up, “ABANDON SHIP!”
They manned the lifeboats, rowed away
And lived to sail another day.
I’m very pleased to tell you that
The Great Explorer saved the cat.

But what about the little bird,
Who's rarely seen and seldom heard?
The cage blew open, out it came,
It found some wood amongst the flame,
It floated off, through waves and foam,
Back to its sunny island home.
And ever since that fateful day,
When sailing ships have passed their way,
The sailors walking through their zone
Have left the little birds alone.

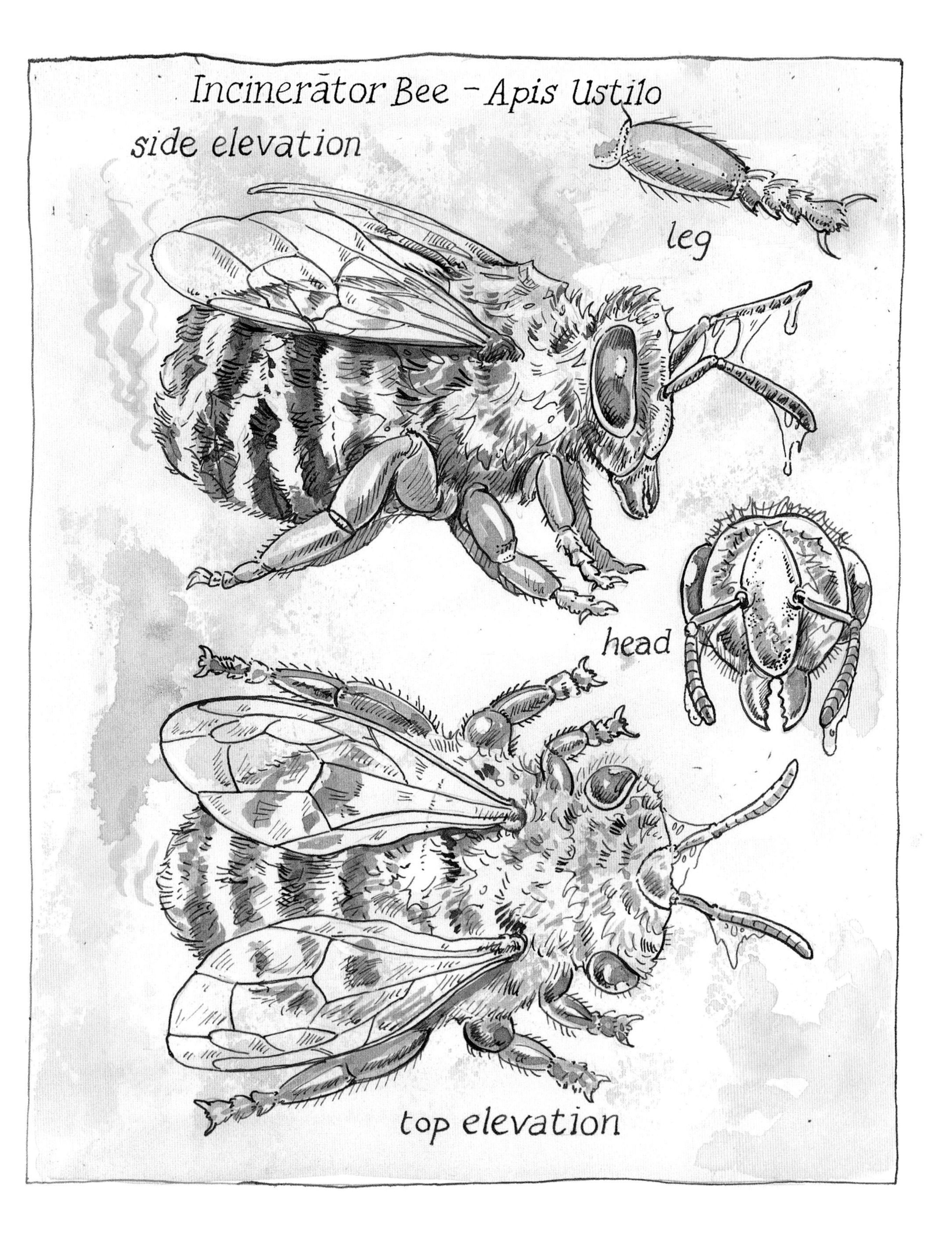
Incinerātor Bee - Apis Ustilo
side elevation
leg
head
top elevation

# The Incinerator Bee

No stranger creature will you see
Than an Incinerator Bee.
It's small and hairy, clumsy too
And covered in a sticky goo,
With stripes of gold and jungle green
And with a smell that's quite obscene
(Your trumps are whiffy, so you think –
They're not as bad as this bee's stink!)
It has another nasty feature,
Making it a deadly creature.
If you see one please beware –
You must approach it with great care…

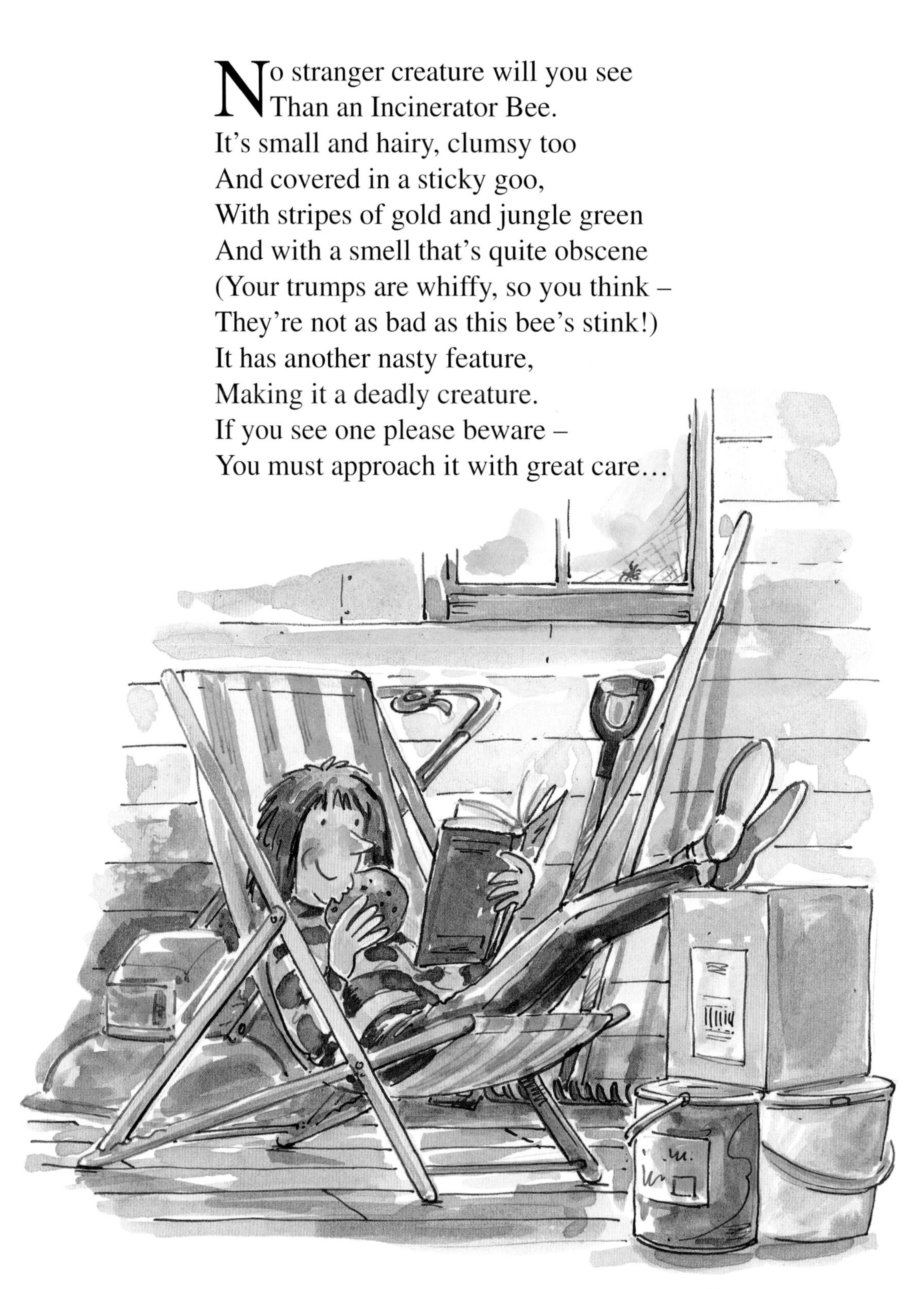

One bright and sunny summer's day
My mother said, "Go out to play,"
But in my normal lazy way
I went to hide myself away.
I took a book I hadn't read
Down to my father's garden shed.
I'd read as far as chapter one
(Whilst munching on a currant bun)
When high-pitched humming filled the air –
I felt vibrations through my chair.
Accompanying this as well
Was quite the most disgusting smell.
It stank of sulphur laced with dregs
And dog poop mixed with rancid eggs.
I saw a movement from the shed
In father's little flower bed
And, putting down my reading book,
I went to take a closer look.
The thing that had upset my nose
Was sitting there upon a rose,
Humming in amongst the blooms
Whilst spreading its revolting fumes,
Shimmering with gold and green
And reeking like an old latrine!
I thought the bee looked very funny,
Getting nectar for its honey.
I gave it just a little poke –
I only did it for a joke –

But, if you live a life that's long,
You won't get anything more wrong!

Instead of stinging you, you'll find
That flames shoot out from its behind.
They fly out in a fiery shower,
Burning with tremendous power.
Spreading wide and glowing bright
They're apt to set your clothes alight.

So, when you smell its dreadful stink,
Please make sure that you stop to think
And when you hear its high-pitched hum,
Beware the fire from its bum!
You mustn't tease this fearsome bee –
Just look at what it did to me!

Chikimunki Marmoset - Simia Bucculentus
front elevation
foot
hand
back elevn
mouth

# The Chikimunki Marmoset

If you are mad enough to get
A Chikimunki Marmoset
And try to keep it as a pet,
It will be something you'll regret!
This little monkey has, you see,
A doctorate and Ph.D.
In Naughtiness and Trickery
From Oxford University.
Although, no doubt, you'll think it cute,
It is a most uncaring brute.
It simply doesn't give a hoot,
So I urge you to follow suit!

I found one sitting in a tree.
It looked as sweet as sweet could be.
I picked it up and, foolishly,
I took the creature home with me.
Of course, it wasn't long before
I came to see what lay in store.
This little scoundrel, just for kicks,
Amused itself by playing tricks!
My bath was filled with rusty nails;
My bedroom teemed with garden snails;
My supper swarmed with slimy slugs;
My playhouse crawled with creepy bugs.

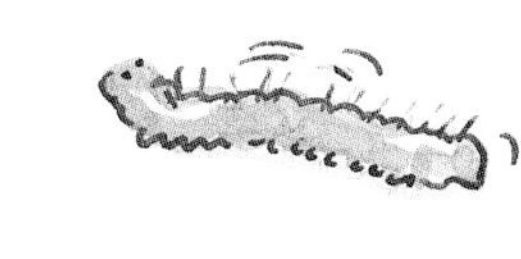

And then things went from bad to worse –
The little beast became a curse.
Sharp tacks were strewn beneath my feet;
It bubble-gummed me to my seat;
It filled my bed with soldier ants;
Put itching powder in my pants;
It pinched my bum and ran away –
Oh boy, this rascal had to pay!

I vowed to get things back on track
And pay the little villain back.
When this was done I surely would
Remove it from my neighbourhood.

I hatched myself a fiendish plan
And commandeered my father's van.
To help me get the little dope
I found a ladder and some rope.
I parked beside its favourite tree
And climbed the ladder, carefully.
I tied the rope, I found an axe,
Then carpeted the ground with tacks.

Next up I filled a water pail
And hung it from my curtain rail.
I primed it with a piece of thread,
Then went to lie down on my bed.
Through my window in it crept,
While I pretended that I slept,
Then, joyfully, I pulled the thread
And tipped the water on its head.

The Chikimunki Marmoset
Is terrified of getting wet
And howled with fright at being soaked
(You must agree, I'd been provoked!)

I struggled to contain my glee
As it sought refuge in its tree.
I dashed downstairs into the van
To execute my cunning plan.

At breakneck speed my vehicle went;
Down to the grass the tree was bent.
The creature couldn't jump to ground
As tacks were lying all around.

I stopped the van; I grabbed the axe;
I stumbled in the tyre tracks;
I chopped the piece of rope in two –
The tree sprang upwards, right on cue.

Through the air the creature flew.
It did a somersault or two,
Then sailed into the city zoo
And landed in a pile of poo.

I punched the air, I shouted, "**YES!**"
I celebrated my success.
I ran in circles like a loon…
I'd celebrated FAR too soon!

As I stepped through the kitchen door
I tripped and fell towards the floor.
I hadn't seen the piece of string –
A tripwire left by The Thing.
I fell – and this is not a lie –
Headfirst into a cowpat pie
And, as I wiped it from my eye,
I gave a long and weary sigh.

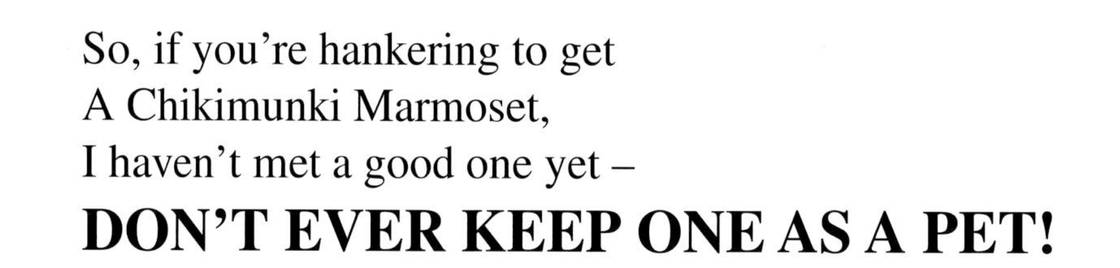

So, if you're hankering to get
A Chikimunki Marmoset,
I haven't met a good one yet –
**DON'T EVER KEEP ONE AS A PET!**

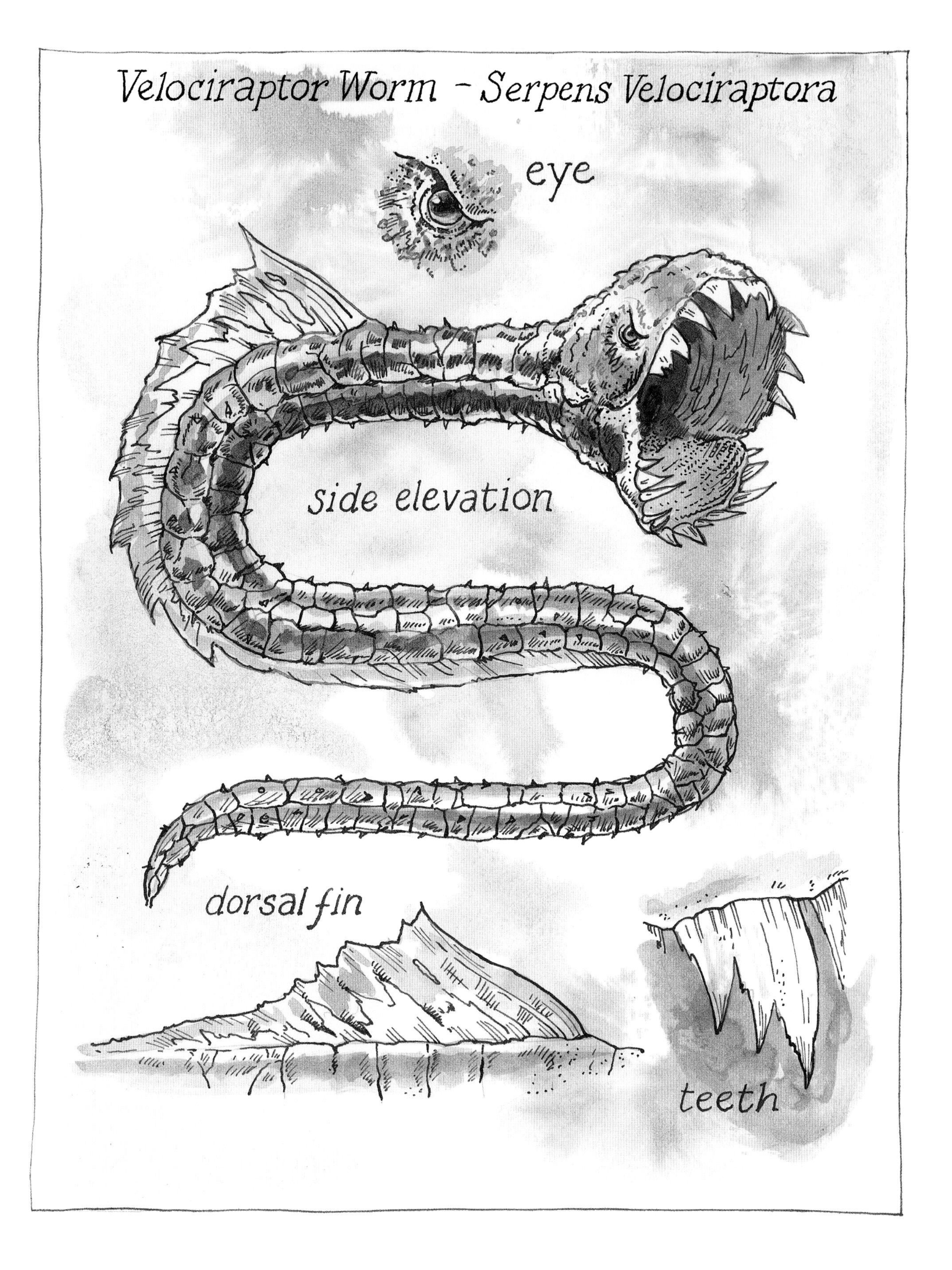
Velociraptor Worm - Serpens Velociraptora
eye
side elevation
dorsal fin
teeth

# The Velociraptor Worm

A fierce Velociraptor Worm
Is guaranteed to make you squirm.
If one comes to your house for tea
It is the last thing you will see…

Velociraptor Worms are found
A thousand feet below the ground
And you'll think that is just as well
Because they seem to come from Hell!

They have a most ferocious bite
And a voracious appetite
(The things these creatures like to eat
Are always made of blood and meat).
Their crusty, armour-plated skin
Has, on its top, a dorsal fin,
Which means these gruesome worms can swim
Through red-hot lava on a whim.

Just like the earthworms in your grass
Their healing powers are first class –
If you should cut one clean in half
A new head grows, both fore and aft,
So when you think its life is through
You'll find that you've created two.

Now one day, many years ago,
Some slithered from a lava flow
While it was spreading, hot and slow,
From an erupting volcano.
As they traversed the isle of Crete
They looked for things that they could eat…

And that was how it came about
That the Minoans all died out.
Historians don't think this so,
But what do silly scholars know?
No explanation could be found
So they assumed the people drowned
When a tsunami hit the land –
But this assumption should be canned!
No information could they find
Because the worms don't leave behind
The slightest little teensy trace
Of evidence about the place.

Ignoring victims' wails and moans
They eat their flesh and leave their bones;
They make sure that their meal's complete
By guzzling every scrap of meat;
They scoff up everything in sight
Then disappear into the night.

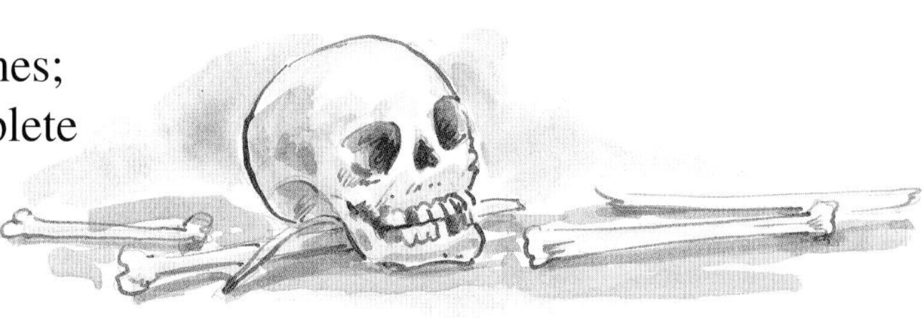

So, have you ever stopped to think
Why dinosaurs became extinct?
Or why a prehistoric man
Should end up as an also-ran?
Or why the mammoths, dodo birds
And other things of which we've heard,
That roamed the earth, untamed and free,
Should all die out so suddenly?

It is my firmly held belief
That answers surely lie beneath
The crust that forms this planet's land –
The very ground on which you stand.
So, if you're travelling one day,
Through fiery mountains far away,
When red-hot lava starts to flow
Then flee as fast as you can go.
You look so nice to chomp and chew
Those worms would like to eat you too…

Curious Creatures Support

each
East Anglia's Children's Hospices
Providing care + support EACH step of the way

# East Anglia's Children's Hospices (EACH)

**East Anglia's Children's Hospices (EACH)**
supports families and cares for children and young people with life-threatening conditions across Cambridgeshire, Essex, Norfolk and Suffolk.

**At EACH**
our care and support is tailored for the needs of all family members and delivered where the families wish – in their own home, at hospital, in the community or at one of three hospices in Ipswich, Milton and Quidenham.

*"Charlie has day care and overnight stays. It means we can have a break and he gets the best possible care. Nurses come to our home too, which means we can relax at home and catch up on much-needed sleep, knowing Charlie is being well cared for."*

**Cheryl – Charlie's mum**

*"One of the best things about the hospice is the parent and toddler group. We're able to discuss things that are relevant to us as parents of children with different needs to other children.*

*"Having a child with complex health problems can leave you feeling like an outsider but when we're at the hospice and we see all the other families in similar situations it helps us to know we're not alone."*

**Helen – William's mum**

**Caring for a child or young person**
with a life-threatening illness, often for 24 hours a day seven days a week, can put a huge strain on family life which can become governed by the timetable of nursing and medical needs.

We deliver a wide range of services through short-break care, emotional and psychological support, symptom management, care at end of life, bereavement support and many activities and therapies.

*EACH – Registered Charity Number 1069284*

*Royal Patron: HRH The Duchess of Cambridge*